This Little Tiger book belongs to:

_____

_____

_____

Extra Wriggly Worms

For Mark, Anna and Charlotte
with my love – T C

To Laura, Grace and Oscar
for putting up with Trolls in the house
– L W

**Daily Mail**

Little Tiger Press
An imprint of Magi Publications
1 The Coda Centre, 189 Munster Road,
London SW6 6AW • www.littletigerpress.com
First published in Great Britain 2010
This edition published 2010
Text copyright © Tracey Corderoy 2010
Illustrations copyright © Lee Wildish 2010
Tracey Corderoy and Lee Wildish have asserted their rights
to be identified as the author and illustrator of this work
under the Copyright, Designs and Patents Act, 1988
A CIP catalogue record for this book is available
from the British Library • All rights reserved
ISBN 978-1-84895-051-1 • Printed in Singapore
10 9 8 7 6 5 4 3 2 1

Mouldy
wet Big
Bogeys

LITTLE TIGER PRESS
London

Tracey
Corderoy

Lee
Wildish

# THE GRUNT AND THE GROUCH

The Grunt was probably
the grumpiest troll you'd *ever* be
likely to meet. Just look at his face!
Now tell me – would you invite *him* to your
party? Well, one day someone did just that.
And things were never quite the same again . . .

It happened on a Tuesday – the most *boring* day of the week –
this scrappy bit of paper landed on The Grunt's dirty doormat . . .
"What's this?" he cried, snatching it up.
So he read the scruffy writing . . .

KEEP
OUT!

"Who's **dared** leave this on my mat?"
growled The Grunt.
"I **don't** like Tuesdays. I **don't** like visitors.
And I **really don't** like parties . . .
so I'm not coming!"

With that, he tore the invitation
into tiny shreds, then stomped back
inside and finally got to work . . .

Boring Tuesday morning ended and boring Tuesday
afternoon began. So The Grunt went to town –
it was, after all, the perfect place . . .

Shake and bake

...to be horrid!

So he **jumped** in
muddy puddles . . .

**growled** at
kitty cats . . .

and **swiped** a teddy from
every pram he saw!

CLICK CLACK
CLOCKS

PUB

When the postman smiled, "Good afternoon!"
"No it's not!" grumped The Grunt.
Then posted him (without sticking
on any stamps!).

Back home, as The Grunt thundered in through his gate, who should he find but a visitor!

"Grrrrrr!" he bellowed. "I'm The Grunt! No one parties in my garden!"

HOME SWEET HOME

Coke

BOGEY JUICE

WET WORMS

Bang!   Bang!   Bang!

He waved a dirty fingernail.
"Now clear off!" he snarled.
Then **bang – bang – bang** went the pretty balloons
as The Grunt popped every one!

"Oi – party pooper!" snapped The Grouch.
"You great big grunty **grump!**"
Then he chucked a chunk of
his pongiest cheese . . .

And that's when the food

fight began.

"Hang on a minute . . ." said The Grunt.
"Those maggot-cakes look great!"
So they sat and ate and The Grunt had such fun
he forgot to be mean . . . he forgot to be *bored* and
he *even* forgot to send The Grouch away!

"Now . . ." burped The Grunt.
"What **else** can we do?"

"Troll stuff!" cried The Grouch.

So they **messed around** with spots and **goo** . . .

SMALL ONES

BIG bogeys

Medium bogeys

took turns to **cheat** at

a game or two . . .

and hid from the sunshine . . .
**together!**

A whole week later, The Grouch packed up his tent.
"Oh well, Grunty," he sighed. "It's been great!
But now I must go. See – I always
move garden on a Tuesday . . ."

"But . . . *why?*" said The Grunt. And then he saw it —
the tiny troll looked . . . *sad.* The Grunt had never
seen sad before. What's more, he'd never cared!
But now . . . suddenly . . . he did.

"You asked me why I go," said The Grouch,
disappearing through the gate. "I go because . . .
no one's ever asked me to stay."

The Grunt sat and thought, then . . .
"**Wait!**" he cried, tearing off after his friend.
"Grouchy – hey – come back!" he called.
"It won't be the same without *you!*"

KEEP OUT!

UNWELCOME

But where was The Grouch?
He'd disappeared! So The Grunt
searched high and low.

He raced. He chased.
He dashed. He crashed!

And then, at last . . .

...he **found him!**
"Grouchy – stay!" panted The Grunt.
"Wow – thanks . . ." sniffed the little Grouch.

Then The Grunt felt his lips go all tickly
and begin to curl up to his ears . . .
"What's this?" he said. It felt *so good!*
And The Grouch cried, "I think we're **smiling!**"

HERE THERE

Now The Grunt and The Grouch are the **happiest** trolls you'd ever be likely to meet!

Still they **never** pick bits of mould off their teeth . . .

**Never** clean the bath . . .

**Never** do the washing up . . .

And never, ever, EVER flush the toilet!

But, every Tuesday, they get dressed up.
Now it's their **favourite** day!
For that's the day . . .

# You'll never be **grouchy** with these books from Little Tiger Press!

Sylvia and Bird
Catherine Rayner

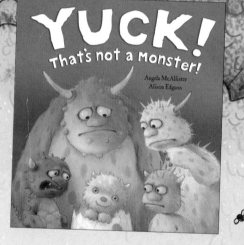

YUCK!
That's not a Monster!
Angela McAllister
Alison Edgson

Rhino's Great BIG Itch!
Natalie Chivers

PAUL BRIGHT
CHARLIE'S SUPERHERO
Lee Wildish

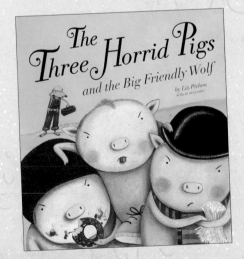

The Three Horrid Pigs
and the Big Friendly Wolf
by Liz Pichon
who is very nice

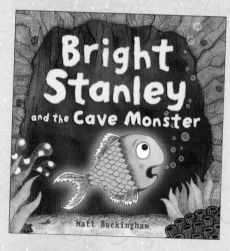

Bright Stanley
and the Cave Monster
Matt Buckingham

For information regarding any of the above titles or for our catalogue, please contact us:
Little Tiger Press, 1 The Coda Centre, 189 Munster Road, London SW6 6AW
Tel: 020 7385 6333 • Fax: 020 7385 7333 • E-mail: info@littletiger.co.uk • www.littletigerpress.com